CareBears™
THE FIRST DAY OF CARING SCHOOL

Written by Sonia Sander
Illustrated by Saxton Moore

Designed by Michael Massen

No part of this publication may be reproduced in whole or in part, or stored in a retrieval system, or transmitted in any form or by any means, electronic, mechanical, photocopying, recording, or otherwise, without written permission of the publisher. For information regarding permission, write to Scholastic Inc., Attention: Permiss'

ISBN 0-439-88557-4

12 11 10 9 8 7 6 5 4 3 2 1
Printed in the U.S.A. First printing, Se

D1399966

SCHOLASTIC INC.
New York   Toronto   London   Auckland   Sydney
Mexico City   New Delhi   Hong Kong   Buenos Aires

Today was the first day of caring school. Share Bear was a little nervous.

"I hope I didn't forget to bring anything," she said.

Share Bear's school bag was much bigger than her friends' bags.

"It looks like you brought everything you need," smiled Love-a-lot Bear.

"Welcome to school!" said Tenderheart Bear.
"I hope you are all ready to share in some fun."

Share Bear knew she was.

Tenderheart Bear asked the
Care Bears to take out a pencil.

Share Bear was the only one who had one.

In fact, Share Bear had enough pencils for the entire class!

She gave one pencil to each Care Bear.

In the end, Share Bear gave all of her pencils away. She didn't have a pencil for herself.

Luckily, Tenderheart Bear had an extra pencil to share with her.

At snack time, Share Bear had more to share.

She shared cupcakes with the whole class.

She shared so many that she only had crumbs left for herself.

Luckily, Friend Bear split her cupcake into two pieces and gave one of them to Share Bear.

At naptime, Share Bear helped Bedtime Bear.

She gave out pillows and blankets.

She even shared her favorite book.

The whole class loved Share Bear's book.

But Share Bear was too sleepy to listen to the story.

She fell right to sleep as soon as
Bedtime Bear started to read.

In art class, Share Bear shared her picture.

"My favorite part of today was sharing it with all of you," she said.

At the end of the day, Tenderheart Bear asked the Care Bears what they had learned.

Funshine Bear raised his hand.
"Today we learned that sharing with friends
is the most important thing!"

When class was finished, Share Bear packed up and headed home.

"Share Bear, if you shared all day, why is your school bag so full?" Love-a-lot Bear asked.

"All of my friends thanked me for sharing with them today!" answered Share Bear. "My bag is full of thank-you notes!"